THE LITERARY BOOK

OF ANSWERS™

THE LITERARY BOOK OF ANSWERS™

CAROL BOLT

NEW YORK

LIBRARY OF CONGRESS CATALOGING-IN-PUBLICATION DATA

THE LITERARY BOOK OF ANSWERS / [COMPILED BY] CAROL BOLT.
    P. CM.
   ISBN 0-7868-6699-3
    1. FORTUNE-TELLING BY BOOKS. 2. QUOTATIONS, ENGLISH—MISCELLANEA.
I. BOLT, CAROL, 1963–

BF1891.B66 L58 2000
133.3—DC21

00-040715

FIRST EDITION
10 9 8 7 6 5 4 3 2 1

HOW TO USE
THE LITERARY BOOK OF ANSWERS™

1. HOLD THE **CLOSED** BOOK IN YOUR HAND, ON YOUR LAP, OR ON A TABLE.

2. TAKE 10 OR 15 SECONDS TO **CONCENTRATE** ON YOUR QUESTION.
   QUESTIONS SHOULD BE PHRASED **CLOSED-END**, E.G., "IS THE JOB I'M
   APPLYING FOR THE RIGHT ONE?" OR "SHOULD I TRAVEL THIS WEEKEND?"

3. WHILE VISUALIZING OR SPEAKING YOUR QUESTION (ONE QUESTION
   AT A TIME), PLACE **ONE HAND** PALM DOWN ON THE BOOK'S FRONT COVER
   AND **STROKE THE EDGE** OF THE PAGES, BACK TO FRONT.

4. WHEN YOU **SENSE** THE TIME IS RIGHT, **OPEN** THE BOOK AND
   THERE WILL BE YOUR ANSWER.

5. **REPEAT** THE PROCESS FOR AS MANY QUESTIONS AS YOU HAVE.

GOT QUESTIONS? THIS BOOK HAS THE ANSWERS.

CAROL BOLT IS A PROFESSIONAL ARTIST LIVING IN SEATTLE.
SHE IS ALSO THE AUTHOR OF *THE BOOK OF ANSWERS*™.

THE LITERARY BOOK
OF ANSWERS™

THE FACTS WILL APPEAR
WITH THE SHINING
OF THE DAWN.

—Aeschylus: *Agamemnon*

DON'T TRY TO BEND
A STUBBORN HEART.

—Sappho: *A Garland*

YOU SHOULD MAKE
A LIVING OUT OF THAT.

—Langston Hughes: *Not Without Laughter*

THAT [WOULD BE] THY LOSS.

—Rudyard Kipling: *The Jungle Book*

DON'T CONSULT ANYONE'S OPINIONS BUT YOUR OWN.

—Aulus Persius Flaccus: *Satires*

ASSUME YOU SHALL ASSUME.

—Walt Whitman: "Song of Myself"

TAKE CARE OR
THE DOG WILL BARK.

—Unknown Chinese poet: *Book of Songs*

GRACEFULLY TURN BACK
YOUR THOUGHTS.

—Veronica Gambara: "Sonnet 24"

PICK FROM A HIGHER BUSH
AND A SWEETER BERRY.

—Zora Neale Hurston:
Their Eyes Were Watching God

ARRIVE SAFELY.

—Anne Frank: *The Diary of a Young Girl*

[IT IS] AGAINST GOOD CUSTOM.

—Seneca: *Dialogues*

BETTER BEANS AND BACON
IN PEACE THAN
CAKE AND ALE IN FEAR.

—Aesop: "The Town Mouse and the Country Mouse"

IT IS NOT POSSIBLE,
YOUR NOTION MUST BE WRONG.

—Homer: *The Odyssey*

LET YOUR COMPASSION
BE MOVED.

—Mary Wollstonecraft Shelley:
Frankenstein

WHERE ALL IS PLAIN THERE IS NOTHING TO BE ARGUED.

—Frederick Douglass:
The Life and Writings of Frederick Douglass

SOMETHING IS ROTTEN
IN THE STATE OF DENMARK.

—William Shakespeare: *Hamlet*

BEAR "TIT FOR TAT" IN MIND.

—John Aikin: "A Tale"

YOU ARE THE FAVOURED POSSESSOR OF THE BENEFICIENT FAIRY.

—Emily Bronte: *Wuthering Heights*

IT IS NOUGHT GOOD
A SLEPYNG HOUND TO WAKE.

—Geoffrey Chaucer: *Troilus and Criseyde*

THAT SEEMS TO HAVE A STAMP OF TRUTH UPON IT.

—Oscar Wilde: *The Importance of Being Earnest*

SEW YOURSELF UP IN IT.

—Herman Melville: *Billy Budd*

NEVER.

—Ernest Hemingway:
For Whom the Bell Tolls

JOKING DECIDES GREAT THINGS.

—John Milton: *Imitation of Horace*

ACCEPT A MIRACLE.

—Edward Young: *Anecdotes*

KEEP UP APPEARANCES, WHATEVER YOU DO.

—Charles Dickens: *Martin Chuzzlewit*

IT'S SILLY.

—Lucy Maud Montgomery:
Anne of Green Gables

CONTRIVE REASONS FOR DELAY.

—Virgil: *Aeneid*

CERTAINLY.

—Leo Tolstoy: *Anna Karenina*

LIVE ALL YOU CAN;
IT'S A MISTAKE NOT TO.

—Henry James: *The Ambassadors*

SOMETIMES IT IS A GOOD CHOICE
NOT TO CHOOSE AT ALL.

—Michel Eyquem de Montaigne: *Essays*

AN INQUIRY WILL AFFORD [YOU] AMUSEMENT.

—Edgar Allan Poe:
"The Murders in the Rue Morgue"

A PLEASANT COMPANION
WILL REDUCE THE
LENGTH OF THE JOURNEY.

—Publilius Syrus: *Maxims*

BE CONTENT WITH YOUR LOT.

—Aesop: "The Peacock and Juno"

DO JUST AS YOU MAY PLEASE, FOR MY BEST JUDGMENT WITH YOUR OWN AGREES.

—Geoffrey Chaucer: *The Canterbury Tales*

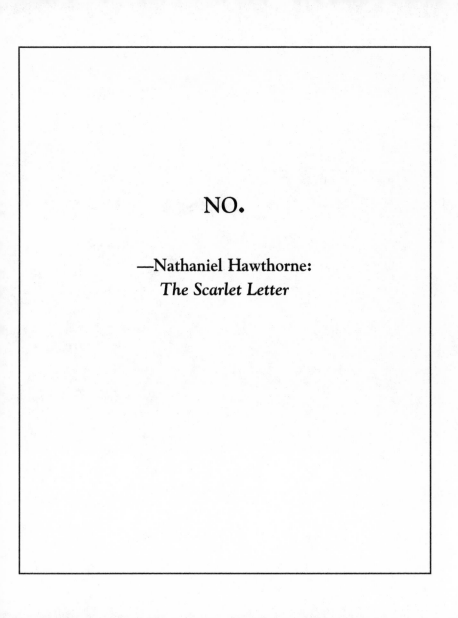

NO.

—Nathaniel Hawthorne:
The Scarlet Letter

MIGHT BE HAPPY
ALL THE SAME THAT WAY.

—James Joyce: *Ulysses*

WHEN THE TIME'S RIGHT.

—Marguerite of Navarre: *Heptaméron*

YOU WILL SEE PROOF
OF THIS VERY SHORTLY.

—Plato: *Symposium*

CUDGEL THY BRAINS NO MORE ABOUT IT.

—William Shakespeare: *Hamlet*

HAVE THE COURAGE TO DARE.

—Fyodor Dostoyevsky: *Crime and Punishment*

SO GOODLY ALL AGREE
WITH SWEET CONSENT.

—Edmund Spenser: *Epithalamion*

THERE'S NO BREAD
WITHOUT LEAVENING.

—Gustave Flaubert: *Journal*

HANDLE YOUR TOOLS
WITHOUT MITTENS.

—Benjamin Franklin: *Poor Richard's Almanack*

GREAT GUNS, THIS IS A GO!

—Mark Twain: *The Adventures of Huckleberry Finn*

BE A GOOD ANIMAL,
TRUE TO YOUR INSTINCTS.

—D. H. Lawrence: *The White Peacock*

LET BE
WHAT COMES TOMORROW.

—Horace: *Odes*

YOU'D BETTER NOT DO THAT AGAIN!

—Lewis Carroll: *Alice's Adventures in Wonderland*

IT IS A TRUTH UNIVERSALLY ACKNOWLEDGED.

—Jane Austen: *Pride and Prejudice*

PAY THY SCORE
WITHOUT MORE ADO.

—Howard Pyle: *The Merry Adventures of Robin Hood*

I DO PERCEIVE HERE
A DIVIDED DUTY.

—William Shakespeare: *Othello*

THAT FIXES IT!

—Robert Louis Stevenson: *Treasure Island*

SPECULATIONS ARE PROFITLESS.

—Oscar Wilde: *The Importance of Being Earnest*

PREPARE! YOUR TOILS ONLY BEGIN.

—Mary Wollstonecraft Shelley: *Frankenstein*

BE CONTENT WITH THAT.

—Charles Perrault: *Complete Fairy Tales*:
"Beauty and the Beast"

YOU CANNOT GO WITH YOUR
PITCHER TO THIS FOUNTAIN.

—Herman Melville: *Moby-Dick*

WHAT DO YOU WANT?

—Victor Hugo: *Les Misérables*

YES.

—Nathaniel Hawthorne:
The Scarlet Letter

FLOW BACKWARD
TO YOUR SOURCES.

—**Euripides:** *Medea*

PRESUME NOTHING.

—Sir Arthur Conan Doyle:
The Hound of the Baskervilles

WAIVE THAT A MOMENT AND ASK ANOTHER.

—Charles Dickens: *Great Expectations*

CLEAR THE GROUND
THAT [YOU] MAY.

—James Fenimore Cooper: *The Pioneers*

SPARE YOUR BREATH
TO COOL YOUR PORRIDGE.

—Miguel de Cervantes: *Don Quixote*

COUNT THE WAYS.

—Elizabeth Barrett Browning:
"The Lady's Yes"

LIKE A DOG . . .
HUNT IN [YOUR] DREAMS.

—Alfred, Lord Tennyson: "Locksley Hall"

HARP NOT ON THAT STRING.

—William Shakespeare: *Richard III*

GO WITH THE CURRENT.

—Ovid: *The Art of Love*

ONE SHOULD ALWAYS
HAVE ONE'S BOOTS ON,
AND BE READY TO LEAVE.

—Michel Eyquem de Montaigne: *Essays*

[GIVE IT] THE TRIBUTE OF A PAUSE AND STARE.

—Herman Melville: *Billy Budd*

NO GUTS IN IT.

—James Joyce: *Ulysses*

PLUNGE IN
BOTH YOUR HANDS.

—Amy Lowell: *What's O'Clock*

SEIZE THE DAY (CARPE DIEM).

—Horace: *Odes*

CAN'T SPECK TER KNOW
ALL 'BOUT EVE'YTHING
'FO' [YOU] GIT SOME RES'.

—Joel Chandler Harris:
The Complete Tales of Uncle Remus:
"Mr. Terrapin Appears upon the Scene"

YOU SEEM TO HAVE YOUR
MIND QUITE MADE UP.

—Henry James: *The Story of a Year*

END WITH LOTS OF
BIRTHDAY CAKE.

—Katherine Mansfield: "A Joyful Song of Five"

FULL COUNSEL MUST MATURE.

—John Milton: *Paradise Lost*

THE THINGS THAT HEAVEN MADE [YOU WERE] MEANT TO USE.

—Li T'ai Po: "Chiang Chin Chiu"

RIDE YOUR WAYS.

—Sir Walter Scott: *Guy Mannering*

THROW MUD ON THIS.

—Sophocles: *Oedipus Rex*

THERE IS A REASON THAT ALL THINGS ARE AS THEY ARE.

—Bram Stoker: *Dracula*

A THOUSAND PENS
ARE READY TO SUGGEST
WHAT YOU SHOULD DO.

—Virginia Woolf: *A Room of One's Own*

OUT UPON YOUR GUARDED LIPS!

—Ralph Waldo Emerson: *Essays*

BETTER AIN'T TO BE GOT!

—Charles Dickens: *Great Expectations*

IF IT WAS SO, IT MIGHT BE;
AND IF IT WERE SO,
IT WOULD BE;
BUT AS IT ISN'T, IT AIN'T.

—Lewis Carroll: *Through the Looking Glass*

YOU'SE TAKIN'
UH MIGHTY BIG CHANCE.

—Zora Neale Hurston:
Their Eyes Were Watching God

GIVE UP THE SPEAR!

—Herman Melville: *Moby-Dick*

DO WHAT THOU WILT.

—Francois Rabelais: *Gargantua*

TIME FOR A LITTLE SOMETHING.

—A. A. Milne: *Winnie-the-Pooh*

THAT'S A MOOT POINT.

—Oscar Levant: *A Smattering of Ignorance*

EXPERIENCE KEEPS
A DEAR SCHOOL.

—Benjamin Franklin:
preface to *Poor Richard's Almanack*

NOW AND IN TIME TO BE.

—William Butler Yeats: "Easter 1916"

THERE IS NO ARMOR
AGAINST FATE.

—James Shirley:
Contention of Ajax and Ulysses

ALL THINGS FLOURISH
WHERE YOU TURN YOUR EYES.

—Alexander Pope: *Pastorals*

WAIT A LITTLE.

—Rudyard Kipling: *Rikki-Tikki-Tavi*

THE GODS THOUGHT OTHERWISE.

—Virgil: *Aeneid*

MAKE HAY
WHILE THE SUN SHINES.

—Miguel de Cervantes: *Don Quixote*

YOU'VE PUT YOUR
FOOT IN IT NOW.

—Louisa May Alcott: *Jo's Boys*

DO NOT LOOK . . .
ONLY LISTEN.

—Victor Hugo:
The Hunchback of Notre Dame

LISTEN TO REASON.

—George Bernard Shaw: *Man and Superman*

THERE FIX THY VIEW.

—Phillis Wheatley: "To a Lady
on the Death of Her Husband"

PASS ONWARD WITHOUT DRAWING NIGH TO IT.

—Dante Alighieri: *The Divine Comedy*

THAT IS INDISPUTABLE.

—Voltaire: *Candide*

DON'T FORCE THE GATES.

—Aristophanes: *Lysistrata*

THINK THE FIRST STRAY HORSE AN INDICATION OF PROVIDENCE.

—Harriet Beecher Stowe: *Uncle Tom's Cabin*

[YOU CAN] NOT GET THE RING
WITHOUT THE FINGER.

—Thomas Middleton: *The Changeling*

JUST DON'T DAWDLE IN BED.

—Franz Kafka: *The Metamorphosis*

OF COURSE.

—F. Scott Fitzgerald: "Babylon Revisited"

SHIFT THE PEGS A LITTLE.

—George Eliot (Mary Ann Evans):
Middlemarch

BURROW A WHILE
AND BUILD, BROAD
ON THE ROOTS OF THINGS.

—Robert Browning: "Abt Vogler"

I DO NOT KNOW WHAT
TO ANSWER TO THAT.

—Jules Verne: *20,000 Leagues Under the Sea*

SO BE IT.

—Plato: *Phaedo* (attr. Socrates)

WELCOME ANYTHING
THAT COMES TO YOU,
BUT DO NOT LONG FOR
ANYTHING ELSE.

—André Gide: *The Fruits of the Earth*

MAKE A LONG STORY SHORT.

—Washington Irving: *Rip Van Winkle*

YOU WILL GO MOST SAFELY
BY THE MIDDLE WAY.

—Ovid: *Metamorphoses*

[BE] THE VERY PINEAPPLE
OF POLITENESS!

—Richard Brinsley Sheridan: *The Rivals*

YOU WILL BE DAMNED
IF YOU DO—AND YOU WILL
BE DAMNED IF YOU DON'T.

—Lorenzo Dow: *Reflections on the Love of God*

YOU MUST GO.

—W. Somerset Maugham: "The Verger"

"THAT" COMES OUT OF "THIS"
AND
"THIS" DEPENDS ON "THAT."

—Chuang Chou: *Chuang Tzu*

EYES OPEN,
PLUNGE DOWN HEADLONG.

—Johann Christoph Friedrich von Schiller:
The Maid of Orleans

YOU'RE JEST MIGHTILY MISTAKEN.

—Hamlin Garland: *The Return of a Private*

DO IT! DO IT!

—Charles Perrault: *Complete Fairy Tales*:
"Sleeping Beauty"

LOOK ASTERN.

—Robert Louis Stevenson: *Treasure Island*

YOU NEED NEW VISTAS.

—Herodas: *Mimiamboi*

YOU [WILL MAKE] A GLORIOUS
LOT OF SMOKE, ANYHOW.

—Joseph Conrad: "Heart of Darkness"

TRY TO GET RID OF IT.

—Franz Kafka: *The Metamorphosis*

THE MOST DIFFICULT WAY
IS IN THE LONG RUN,
THE EASIEST.

—Henry Miller: *The Books in My Life*

NO, NO!

—Sophocles: *Oedipus Rex*

YOU CAN'T TELL
WITHOUT HAVING TRIED IT.

—Leo Tolstoy: *Anna Karenina*

ABSOLUTELY.

—D. H. Lawrence: *Lady Chatterley's Lover*

NOTHING CAN BE
ACTUALLY SETTLED YET,
BUT . . . IT MUST BE
THOUGHT OF.

—Jane Austen: *Emma*

IT WOULD BE EASY TO CLIMB IT.

—Anonymous: "Jack and the Beanstalk"

YOU WON'T NEED MUCH HELP.

—Louisa May Alcott: *Jo's Boys*

NAY, TARRY A MOMENT.

—Pierre-Jean de Beranger:
Le Chasseur et la Latiere

ADD TO WHAT
[YOU'VE] BEEN GIVEN.

—Anton Chekhov: *The Cherry Orchard*

PADDLE HOME.

—Li T'ai-Po: "Autumn River Song"

DON'T MAKE ANY
BONES ABOUT IT.

—Robert Louis Stevenson: *St. Ives*

A LITTLE THING IN THE HAND
IS WORTH MORE THAN
A GREAT THING IN PROSPECT.

—Aesop: "The Fisher and the Little Fish"

LUMP THE WHOLE THING!

—Mark Twain: *The Innocents Abroad*

LISTEN WHERE
THOU ART SITTING.

—John Milton: *Comus*

GUSH FORTH.

—Christopher Marlowe: *Dr. Faustus*

IT IS BETTER FOR YOU NOT TO
KNOW THIS THAN TO KNOW IT.

—Aeschylus: *Prometheus Bound*

YES.

—Hans Christian Andersen:
"In a Thousand Years"

YOU MUST GET [ANOTHER'S] CONSENT BEFORE YOU ASK MINE.

—Jane Austen: *Emma*

DON'T LEAVE IT TO OTHERS.

—Sophocles: *Antigone*

YOU OUGHT TO KNIT UP
A GREAT MATTER WELL.

—Geoffrey Chaucer: *The Canterbury Tales*

[DON'T] PLAY THE ROOSTER
IN FRONT OF
THE WRONG HOUSE.

—Josephina Niggli:
"The Street of the Three Crosses"

THERE [IS] NO HURRY.

—Joseph Conrad: "Heart of Darkness"

THAT IS NOT ENOUGH.

—Confucius: *Book XIII*

MOVE FAST, AND
PUT THE SHIP'S HEAD
TOWARD THE BREAKERS.

—Homer: *The Odyssey*

TAKE SUGGESTION
AS A CAT LAPS MILK.

—William Shakespeare: *The Tempest*

IT'S NOTHING BUT
COMMON SENSE.

—Henry James: *Poor Richard*

CHANGE YOUR IDEAS
OF WHAT YOU WANT.

—Euripides: *Hippolytus*

WHAT IS ORDERED MUST SOONER OR LATER ARRIVE.

—James Fenimore Cooper:
The Last of the Mohicans

WHAT ELSE HAVE YOU GOT IN YOUR POCKET?

—Lewis Carroll:
Alice's Adventures in Wonderland

YES.

—Harriet Beecher Stowe:
Uncle Tom's Cabin

NAY, USE NO FORCE.

—Howard Pyle:
The Merry Adventures of Robin Hood

[YOU WILL] LEARN
THROUGH TRIAL.

—Margaret J. Preston: "Attainment"

WISELY AND SLOW; THEY STUMBLE THAT RUN FAST.

—William Shakespeare: *Romeo and Juliet*

LAUGH—IT IS NOTHING.

—Amy Lowell: *What's O'Clock*

YOU OUGHT TO FOLLOW IT!

—Gustave Flaubert: *Madame Bovary*

THAT IS UNLIKELY.

—Sir Arthur Conan Doyle:
The Hound of the Baskervilles

IS PLENTY!
IS ENOUGH!

—Emily Dickinson: "Life"

SHOW THINGS REALLY
AS THEY ARE.

—Lord Byron: *Don Juan*

AYE!

—Herman Melville: *Moby-Dick*

BETTER COUNSEL
COMES OVERNIGHT.

—Gotthold Ephraim Lessing: *Emilia Galotti*

BETTER LATE THAN NEVER, BUT BETTER NEVER LATE.

—Caroline Spurgeon: *Salt Cellars*

YOU MUST TRAVEL IT
FOR YOURSELF.

—Walt Whitman: "Song of Myself"

DON'T EVEN DISPUTE IT.

—Leo Tolstoy: *Anna Karenina*

LOOK TO YOUR HEALTH.

—Izaak Walton: *The Compleat Angler*

YOU WILL SEE YOUR WAY
CLEARLY ENOUGH.

—George Bernard Shaw: *Man and Superman*

SEE WHAT MONEY WILL DO.

—Samuel Pepys: *Diary*

'TAIN'T WORTH DE TROUBLE.

—Zora Neale Hurston:
Their Eyes Were Watching God

TRY JUST A LITTLE.

—Ernest Hemingway: *The Snows of Kilimanjaro*

EXCELLENT, WATSON, EXCELLENT!

—Sir Arthur Conan Doyle:
The Adventures of Sherlock Homes

SAY WHAT IT IS YOU WANT.

—Aeschylus: *Prometheus Bound*

CEASE YOUR FUNNING.

—John Gay: *The Beggar's Opera*

TURN, NOW,
TO OTHER INDICATIONS.

—Edgar Allan Poe:
"The Murders in the Rue Morgue"

NO NEED OF ALL THIS CAUTION!

—Daniel Defoe: *Robinson Crusoe*

NOBODY KNOWS THAT
BETTER THAN YOU.

—George Eliot (Mary Ann Evans):
Middlemarch

GIVE IT MOUTH!

—Charles Dickens: *Great Expectations*

THINK OF THAT AND PURR.

—Rudyard Kipling:
"How the Leopard Got His Spots"

DIRECT THE CLASPING IVY WHERE TO CLIMB.

—John Milton: *Paradise Lost*

BEWARE OF ENTRANCE
TO A QUARREL.

—William Shakespeare: *Hamlet*

STOP AT THE START.

—Ovid: *Remedia amoris*

[IT] WILL LIFT YOUR TSCHINK WITH TSCHUNK.

—James Joyce: *Ulysses*

IT IS NOT GOOD TO REFUSE.

—Homer: *The Odyssey*

TREAD LIGHTLY.

—Oscar Wilde: "Requiescat"

KEEP A SHARP LOOK-OUT!

—Jules Verne: *20,000 Leagues Under the Sea*

THAT IS BETTER
THAN A CIRCUS!

—Louisa May Alcott: *Jo's Boys*

ABSOLUTELY.

—Anton Chekhov: *Uncle Vanya*

THAT'S A TRAIL NOTHING BUT A NOSE CAN FOLLOW.

—James Fenimore Cooper: *The Last of the Mohicans*

DO IT. BE NOT AFRAID.

—Sophocles: *Oedipus Rex*

COME NOW . . .
TAKE A QUICK TURN.

—Robert Louis Stevenson: *Dr. Jekyll and Mr. Hyde*

CLEAVE EVER TO THE SUNNIER SIDE OF DOUBT.

—Alfred, Lord Tennyson: "The Ancient Sage"

QUICK . . . AIN'T NO TIME
FOR FOOLING AROUND
AND MOANING.

—Mark Twain: *The Adventures of Huckleberry Finn*

BEAT THE GROUND
WITH MEASURED FEET.

—Horace: *Odes*

THOU MUST GATHER
THINE OWN SUNSHINE.

—Nathaniel Hawthorne: *The Scarlet Letter*

THE WAY IS TO BE FOUND.

—Confucius: *Book XVIII*

IT SHALL NOT BE
WITHOUT REWARD.

—Dante Alighieri: *The Divine Comedy*

CHASE [IT] WITH ALL THE
SAIL [YOU] CAN MAKE . . .

—Daniel Defoe: *Robinson Crusoe*

GO FORWARD.

—Euripides: *Andromache*

GET WHAT YOU CAN AND WHAT YOU GET, HOLD.

—Benjamin Franklin: *The Way to Wealth*

FORWARD!

—Victor Hugo: *Les Misérables*

CONTROL YOURSELF.

—Gustave Flaubert: *Madame Bovary*

YONDER LIES SOME MORE
OF THE SAME SORT.

—Hans Christian Andersen:
"The Goblin and the Huckster"

THAT DEPENDS A GOOD DEAL ON
WHERE YOU WANT TO GET TO.

—Lewis Carroll: *Alice's Adventures in Wonderland*

MARAVILLOSA.

—Joseph Conrad: *Nostromo*

NO.

—Emily Brontë: *Wuthering Heights*

DEPEND ON IT, MY DEAR.

—Jane Austen: *Pride and Prejudice*

TRY TO BE HAPPY WITHOUT IT.

—Charles Perrault: *Complete Fairy Tales*:
"Beauty and the Beast"

SWIFT BE THINE
APPROACHING FLIGHT!

—Percy Bysshe Shelley: "To Night"

PERHAPS.

—Gertrude Stein: *How to Write*

O DISCRETION,
THOU ART A JEWEL.

—Unknown

BE STILL.

—Phillis Wheatley: "Ode to Neptune"

ACT WELL
YOUR PART.

—Alexander Pope: "An Essay"

TOMORROW TO FRESH WOODS, AND PASTURES NEW.

—John Milton: "Lycidas"

PERISH THE THOUGHT!

—Colley Cibber: *Richard III*

LIGHTLY IT COMES,
LIGHTLY . . . MAKE IT GO.

—Geoffrey Chaucer: *The Canterbury Tales*

REALLY, I DON'T KNOW.

—Albert Camus: *The Fall*

NO MAN OUGHT TO LOOK
A GIVEN HORSE IN THE MOUTH.

—John Heywood: *Proverbs*

GIT IT WHILE HIT'S FRESH.

—Joel Chandler Harris:
"Brer Rabbit, Brer Fox and the Tar Baby"

TO TURN AND FLY [IS] NOW TOO LATE.

—Washington Irving:
The Legend of Sleepy Hollow

WHITHER DOES YOUR SENSELESS CURIOSITY LEAD YOU?

—Mary Wollstonecraft Shelley: *Frankenstein*

TO THINE OWN SELF BE TRUE.

—William Shakespeare: *Hamlet*

ADOPT THAT COURSE,
IF YOU LIKE.

—Plato: *Symposium*

ALL OR NOTHING.

—Henrik Ibsen: *Brand*

[IF IT] BEGINS IN FEAR
[IT WILL] END IN FOLLY.

—Samuel Taylor Coleridge: *Table Talk*

THROUGH THE UNKNOWN, [YOU'LL] FIND THE NEW.

—Charles Baudelaire: *Les Fleurs du mal*

IT IS THE PART
OF [THE] WISE . . .
NOT [EVEN TO] VENTURE
ALL HIS EGGS IN ONE BASKET.

—Miguel de Cervantes: *Don Quixote*

YOU'LL GET ALL WET FOR NOTHING.

—Fermina Guerra: "Rancho Buena Vista"

IT IS CAUGHT AMONG THE
TANGLES OF YOUR LINE.

—Herman Melville: *Moby-Dick*

ATTENTION MUST BE PAID.

—Arthur Miller: *Death of a Salesman*

GREET THE UNSEEN WITH A CHEER!

—Robert Browning: epilogue to *Asolando*

HIT THE NAIL ON THE HEAD.

—Francis Beaumont and John Fletcher: *Love's Cure*

DOUBT,

OF WHATEVER KIND,

CAN BE ENDED

BY ACTION ALONE.

—Thomas Carlyle: *Past and Present*

YOU MUST MIND YOUR P'S AND Q'S.

—Hannah Cowley: *Who's the Dupe?*

THE GAME IS NOT WORTH THE CANDLE.

—Michel Eyquem de Montaigne: *Essays*

YOU SHALL NOT FAIL.

—Sophocles: *Oedipus Rex*

EXHAUST THE REALM
OF THE POSSIBLE.

—Peter Pindar (Dr. John Wolcot): *Pythian Odes*

IT WILL SERVE AS A SIGN.

—Henry James: "A Tragedy of Error"

GO TO SEEK A
GRAND PERHAPS.

—attributed to François Rabelais on his deathbed

SHORT IN MEASURE, NARROW IN THEME.

—Antipate of Sedoni:
Yesterday Dr. Marcus Went to See the Statue of Zeus

MAYHAP, IT MAY BE SO.

—Howard Pyle:
The Merry Adventures of Robin Hood

YOU WILL FIND IT A VERY GOOD PRACTICE ALWAYS.

—Martin Joseph Routh: in John William Burgon's *Memoir of Dr. Routh*

HOPE IS YOURS.

—Wilfred Owen: "Strange Meeting"

THERE AIN'T GOING TO BE NO TEA.

—Katherine Mansfield: *Journal*

'TIS NO MATTER.

—Christopher Marlowe: *Dr. Faustus*

YOU'LL DO YOURSELF
A MISCHIEF.

—Charles Dickens: *Great Expectations*

[IT WILL] BE LIKE A
BEACON ON THE ROAD
TOWARDS BETTER THINGS.

—Joseph Conrad: "Heart of Darkness"

PATIENCE WILL ACHIEVE MORE THAN FORCE.

—Edmund Burke:
Reflections on the French Revolution

IS *THAT* WHAT YOU WANT?

—James Baldwin: *Another Country*

YOU MAY BE SURE OF THAT.

—Aeschylus: *Prometheus Bound*

THE HEART MUST RULE,
THE HEAD OBEY.

—Francis Davison: *Desire's Government*

IT WILL SOON BE GONE.

—Nathaniel Hawthorne: *The Scarlet Letter*

I THINK [YOU] CAN.

—Watty Piper: *The Little Engine that Could*

DEY AIN' NO SENSE IN IT.

—Mark Twain:
The Adventures of Huckleberry Finn

WITHOUT HASTE,
BUT WITHOUT REST.

—Johann Wolfgang von Goethe: *Zahme Xenien*

NOPE.

—J. D. Salinger: *The Catcher in the Rye*

SCREW YOUR COURAGE TO THE STICKING-PLACE.

—William Shakespeare: *Macbeth*

PROCEED.

—Victor Hugo: *The Hunchback of Notre Dame*

IT'S GOTTA BE.

—Herodas: *Mimiamboi*

YOU'RE NOT UP TO IT, STAY WHERE YOU ARE.

—Anton Chekhov: *The Cherry Orchard*

BOOT, SADDLE, TO HORSE, AND AWAY!

—Robert Browning: "Boot and Saddle"

SIMPLIFY, SIMPLIFY.

—Henry David Thoreau: *Walden*

HEARKEN OTHERWISE.

—Amy Lowell: *What's O'Clock*

LET EVERYTHING RIP.

—James Joyce: *Ulysses*

OPEN IT AND
SEE WHAT'S INSIDE.

—Ralph Ellison: *Invisible Man*

GO,
AND CATCH
A FALLING STAR.

—John Donne: "Go and Catch a Falling Star"

ENJOY IT, ALL OF IT.

—Homer: *The Iliad*

BE BOLD, BE BOLD, AND EVERYWHERE BE BOLD.

—Edmund Spenser: *The Faerie Queene*

BUILD ON YOUR OWN DESERTS.

—Philip Massinger: *A Very Woman*

SCRAMBLE OVER THE OBSTACLES.

—D. H. Lawrence: *Lady Chatterley's Lover*

DO YOUR DUTY, AND LEAVE THE
OUTCOME TO THE GODS.

—Pierre Corneille: *Horace*

IT'S A GOOD THING TO BE FOOLISHLY GAY ONCE IN A WHILE.

—Horace: *The Carmina*

PUSH ON—KEEP MOVING.

—Thomas Morton: *A Cure for the Heartache*

MAKE HASTE!

—Emily Brontë: *Wuthering Heights*

ONE'S GOT TO LIVE, OF COURSE.

—Sidonie-Gabrielle Colette: "The Misfit"

TAKE THE GOODS
THE GODS PROVIDE THEE.

—John Dryden: "Alexander's Feast"

KEEP WHAT YOU HAVE;
THE KNOWN EVIL IS BEST.

—Plautus: *Trinummus*

AS RIGHT AS A TRIVET.

—Oscar Wilde: *The Importance of Being Earnest*

CONSIDER YOUR BEST AND TRUEST INTERESTS.

—Euripides: *Hippolytus*

PINCH YOUR PENNIES.

—Gustave Flaubert: *Madame Bovary*

PAY GREAT ATTENTION.

—Jean de La Bruyère: *Characters*

SIT ON IT A LITTLE
WHILE LONGER.

—Hans Christian Andersen: "The Ugly Duckling"

THAT WOULD BE GRAND, CERTAINLY.

—Lewis Carroll: *Alice's Adventures in Wonderland*

IT IS A FAR, FAR BETTER THING.

—Charles Dickens: *A Tale of Two Cities*

DON'T BE NO LONGER THAN YOU CAN HELP.

—William Faulkner: *As I Lay Dying*

IT IS CLEAR AS YOU OBSERVE.

—Edgar Allan Poe: "The Purloined Letter"

WHATEVER IS, IS RIGHT.

—Alexander Pope: *An Essay on Man*

BETTER BY FAR YOU SHOULD FORGET AND SMILE.

—Christina Georgina Rossetti: "Remember"

FOR WANT OF A NAIL
THE SHOE IS LOST.

—George Herbert: *Jacula Prudentum*

WALLOW IN THESE DELIGHTS.

—George Bernard Shaw: *Man and Superman*

BE UP AND DOING.

—Henry Wadsworth Longfellow:
"A Psalm of Life"

LICK THE HULL KIT-AN'-BOODLE ALL BY YOURSELF.

—Stephen Crane: *The Red Badge of Courage*

IT IS BEST TO PREPARE.

—Aesop: "The Ant and the Grasshopper"

MAKE EVERYTHING SNUG
AND CLOSE,
THAT THE SHIP MIGHT RIDE
AS EASY AS POSSIBLE.

—Daniel Defoe: *Robinson Crusoe*

DON'T JUMP TO CONCLUSIONS.

—Ovid: *The Art of Love*

WATCH IT CAREFULLY.

—Eva March Tappan: "The Stolen Princess"

IT IS NOT THE LIGHT THAT'S NEEDED, BUT THE FIRE.

—Frederick Douglass:
The Life and Writings of Frederick Douglass

MAKE IT A RULE.

—Richard Brinsley Sheridan: *The Critic*

[GET] A GRIP OF THE ESSENTIAL FACTS.

—Sir Arthur Conan Doyle:
The Adventures of Sherlock Holmes

BEGIN WITH THE BEGINNING.

—Lord Byron: *Don Juan*

YOU MAY GO
ANYWHERE YOU WISH.

—Bram Stoker: *Dracula*

YOU'LL SEE IT IN YOUR DREAMS.

—Clinton Scollard: *There Is a Pool on Garda*

THAT WOULD BE
A GOOD SCHEME.

—Jane Austen: *Pride and Prejudice*

LOOK UPON IT AS A REWARD.

—George Eliot (Mary Ann Evans): *Middlemarch*

YOU CANNOT SEE IT,
BUT THROUGH.

—Chuang Chou: *Chuang Tzu*

YOU GOT DE KEYS
TO DE KINGDOM.

—Zora Neale Hurston:
Their Eyes Were Watching God

ENOUGH OR NOT . . .
IT WILL HAVE TO DO.

—Leo Tolstoy: *Anna Karenina*

IT IS CONVENIENT.

—Horatio Alger, Jr.: *Mark, The Match Boy*

EVERYTHING WILL BE SET RIGHT.

—Harriet Beecher Stowe: *Uncle Tom's Cabin*

IT DEPENDS ON YOU.

—Jules Verne: *Around the World in Eighty Days*

DO NOT TRUST THE HORSE, TROJANS!

—Virgil: *Aeneid*

OPEN THY MIND TO THAT
WHICH UNFOLD TO THEE.

—Dante Alighieri: *The Divine Comedy*

HOLD OUT AND FORTIFY.

—Ernest Hemingway: *For Whom the Bell Tolls*

YOU MAY THINK WHAT YOU LIKE AND SAY WHAT YOU THINK.

—Cornelius Tacitus: *Histories*

THERE IS SOMETHING MORE,
I THINK.

—Louisa May Alcott: *Little Women*

SHOW YOUR METTLE.

—Aristophanes: *Lysistrata*

WHEN THE IRON IS WELL HOT, IT WORKETH THE BETTER.

—William Caxton: *Somnes of Aymon*

COMPOSE YOURSELF.

—Robert Louis Stevenson: *Dr. Jekyll and Mr. Hyde*

DO ALL THE GOOD YOU CAN.

—John Wesley: *John Wesley's Rule*

DISTANCE [WOULD] LEND ENCHANTMENT TO THE VIEW.

—Thomas Campbell: *Pleasures of Hope*

TAKE CARE OF THE SENSE,
AND THE SOUNDS WILL
TAKE CARE OF THEMSELVES.

—Lewis Carroll: *Alice's Adventures in Wonderland*

IT IS WORTH MORE
THAN YOU OFFER.

—James Fenimore Cooper: *The Pioneers*

NOTHING TO GET MIXED UP IN.

—F. Scott Fitzgerald: *The Great Gatsby*

PUT OUT NEW BRANCHES.

—Li T'ai Po: "On Kesu Terrace"

ITCH ON PURPOSE
TO BE SCRATCHED.

—Samuel Butler: *Hudibras*

THIS [WILL] BE PLAIN ENOUGH.

—Ralph Waldo Emerson: "Self-Reliance"

LET YOUR OWN DISCRETION BE YOUR TUTOR.

—William Shakespeare: *Hamlet*

FORGET ALL THAT, D'YE SEE WHAT CHARMING WEATHER 'TIS NOW?

—Daniel Defoe: *Robinson Crusoe*

DO NOT ALLOW YOUR EFFORTS TO SLACKEN.

—Confucius: *Book XIII*

IT IS JUST AS WELL!

—Emily Dickinson: "Life"

LEST YOU LOSE THE
SUBSTANCE BY GRASPING
AT THE SHADOW.

—Aesop: "The Dog and the Shadow"

THERE IS SOMETHING AMISS WITH YOUR REASONING.

—Plato: "Apology"

IT IS LOST LABOR TO PLAY
A JIG TO AN OLD CAT.

—Thomas Fuller: *Gnomologia*

IT MEANS A
SHABBY COMPROMISE.

—Henry James: "The Story of a Year"

PULL OUT THE PEG AND
THE LATCH WILL FALL.

—Charles Perrault: *Complete Fairy Tales*:
"Little Red Riding Hood"

YOU HAVE PRECISELY
WHAT YOU DEMAND TO MAKE
[IT] COMPLETE.

—Edgar Allan Poe: "The Purloined Letter"

LISTEN TO THE VOICE OF AN INNOCENT CHILD.

—Hans Christian Andersen:
"The Emperor's New Clothes"

FETTERS OF GOLD
ARE STILL FETTERS.

—Mary Astell: *An Essay in Defence of the Female Sex*

MAKE NO RASH JOURNEYS
ON THESE HILLS.

—Emily Brontë: *Wuthering Heights*

[YOU] WILL ASK MORE QUESTIONS THAN THE WISEST CAN ANSWER.

—Jonathan Swift: *Polite Conversation*

UNSCREW THE LOCKS FROM THE DOORS!

—Walt Whitman: "Song of Myself"

TO BE OF NO USE . . .
THIS IS OF GREAT USE.

—Chuang Chou: *Chuang Tzu*

TAKE THE WORD
OF AN EXPERIENCED HUNTER.

—James Fenimore Cooper:
The Last of the Mohicans

HIT IS NOT AL GOLD, THAT GLARETH.

—Geoffrey Chaucer: *The House of Fame*

[YOU] OWE AS MUCH TO THE BITTER OPPOSITION . . . AS TO THE KINDLY AID.

—Frederick Douglass:
Narrative of the Life of Frederick Douglass

ASK ME NO MORE:
WHAT ANSWER SHOULD I GIVE?

—Alfred, Lord Tennyson: "The Princess"

ACKNOWLEDGMENTS

THIS BOOK IS DEDICATED WITH GRATITUDE AND RESPECT TO:

ALL THE INCLUDED AUTHORS WHO MAKE THE WORDS SEEM TO FLOW SO EASILY . . . THANK YOU FOR SHARING THEM WITH US.

AND TO THE FOLLOWING WRITERS WHO MAKE THEIR ART WITH INTEGRITY, CURIOSITY AND INTELLIGENCE THROUGH WHICH THE REST OF US ARE ABLE TO EXPERIENCE THE WORLD MORE FULLY: BART BAXTER, DORIS A. BOLT, ROBERT G. BOLT, KRIS CALDWELL, DAVE CASERIO, BILLIE CONDON, MARY ELIZABETH CRONIN, ROBERT CUMBOW, TODD DAVIS, JULES REMEDIOS FAYE, MICHAEL HOOD, SANDRA EVERLASTING JONES, DONNI KENNEDY, LANCE LODER, MAUREEN MCLAUGHLIN, MARY PATTON, PAT TAKAYAMA, DIANA TAYLOR AND ERIC KTS WONG.

SPECIAL THANKS TO: KRIS CALDWELL, VICTORIA SANDERS, JENNIFER LANG AND ROBERT CUMBOW.

CHECK OUT THE BOOK OF ANSWERS™ WEBSITE AT *WWW.CAROLBOLT.COM*.